CW00728237

IT WATCHES

Michelle Birbeck

Dedication

To Phill, sorry about putting it on paper for you to relive.

Acknowledgements

With thanks to the team, Phill, Alice, Amy, and its newest member, Cat. I couldn't get all of this done without you all. Thanks for working for free books, drinks, and my eternal gratitude. I promise to keep you supplied in all of those for as long as I can.

IT WATCHES

Eyes of red that screamed and burned glued George to his seat. The heart attack he had been expecting for months was making its way up and down his left arm, clenching his fist as he died. But George barely felt the familiar stabbing. Death was drowned in static and red eyes. Those eyes had plagued him. He couldn't remember when he had first rubbed his eyes and convinced himself that nothing could be staring out of his TV. Visions like that came from one too many drinks

Calling time on his drinking seemed like the way to go, not only to live longer than his doctor gave him, but to stop his imagination from serving him up to the eyes in the television.

The weeks had progressed, however, and the eyes made themselves known more and more often.

Until they triggered something familiar in his chest.

There was no denying it now. No blaming it on a half-bottle of vodka or impending death.

The screen out of which the eyes burned was not only off, but it had been unplugged from the wall for three days.

George's breath came in rapid gasps that rippled his stomach with the effort. Anyone could have been forgiven for thinking he was hiding a pool under the stretched fabric. But had there been a pool, it would have evaporated under the heated glare that was killing him.

Every curse word George knew bounced around inside his skull, looking for a way out. Agony, however, had sewn shut his mouth, so the only screams were those in his head.

Somewhere in the back of George's mind, away from the screaming and cursing, one word whispered: demon.

But the problem with thoughts was that George couldn't change the volume of them. So screams had all the shivering caress of whispers, and that one whispered word had all the impact of an ear-splitting scream.

As the word registered, George knew with absolute certainty that it wouldn't be the heart attack that killed him.

The demon inside his television would get him first.

Shannon's phone was on silent in the bottom of her bag, having been relegated there so she could pay attention to the shopping. The texts could wait, she thought, at least until they were finished.

"Aren't they all the same?" she asked for the fourth time.

"This one has built in FreeView and is HD ready," Radley replied.

"But there's a two hundred quid difference!"

"Which is why I asked what you preferred."

She stared at her husband of eight years with wide eyes and a blank expression. The ringing of his phone cut short his explanation of a bunch of stuff Shannon had no interest in. He rolled his eyes and dragged the phone from his pocket.

He turned away with tense shoulders and wandered a few meters away from Shannon, a finger in one ear and the phone pressed against the other.

The hospital, Shannon thought.

Radley had been at the hospital almost every week for months having various tests to find out what was wrong with him. The call had to be the test results, or an appointment to come in for yet more tests. His hunched shoulders and phone hugging almost always meant bad news.

Shannon turned back to the wall of TVs and tried to focus on the lists of sizes and specs.

Truth be told, she had little interest in getting a new one. Yes, their one had all but exploded and died in a cloud of rank smelling smoke, but everything she wanted to watch was available on the internet anyway.

So why do we need to spend hundreds on a new one? Shannon thought with a shake of her head.

Radley's hand on her shoulder made Shannon jump out of her skin.

"The hospital?" she asked when her heart stopped thundering.

Radley nodded once. "But it's not what you think."

All sorts of possibilities ran through Shannon's mind. Everything from worst case to best case scenarios.

"It's your uncle George."

There is no good time to get a call saying a loved one has died. No one ever has a moment where they look at their called ID and thinks, "Yes, I'd really welcome *that* call right now."

There are, of course, awful   times to get the call. But all things considered, when that particular call comes it's really just varying levels of bad timing.

Shopping for a new TV, surrounded by people going about their daily business doesn't rank very high on the scale of bad times. It does, however, rank well above sitting at home where no one can see you.

For Shannon the call wasn't unexpected. Her uncle George had been ill for some time, but still independent enough to live on his own with only regular visits from a nurse to qualify as care. He was also still young enough to get glared at for his comments when the nurses bent over in front of him.

Still, the words threw her. She blinked once, twice, and ran through the words again.

Slowly, she said, "Okay."

"His nurse found him this morning and took him to the hospital."

Shannon shook herself a little and straightened from a hunch she hadn't realised she was in. "Oh, okay. So he had another heart attack?"

She left off the, "*and he's going to be okay.*"

Somewhere deep down in the back of her mind, the words had all connected and formed the correct conclusion, but the part of her that was fully functioning refused to relinquish to those thoughts. Denial was short lived, however, as the only reason for Radley's tight lips and drawn brow came barrelling through and took over every other thought in Shannon's mind.

"Honey, he was dead before they got to the hospital," Radley was saying, his voice gentle as though speaking the words softly would lessen their impact.

Too late for that. No amount of whispering could undo the damage.

It wasn't as though like the pair had been close. Birthday and Christmas cards every year. Monthly visits that turned to weekly as he grew more ill. They had little in common other than blood, but they were all each other had left. George had married once, divorced, and never married again, and never spoken to his ex-wife, either. Shannon had lost her mother when she was twenty-five, and hadn't seen her father since he walked out of her eight birthday party. As far as family went, Uncle George and Radley were it.

And now just Radley, Shannon thought.

But even as the thought bounced around in her mind, it seemed as though it was being cushioned, as if the bouncing should have been breaking her down and sending tears down her face, but instead she just felt numb, insulated from the crashing around.

The pair left the shop without saying another word, and with each step they took, Shannon felt more alone in the world than ever before.

One week later, two days after Uncle George's funeral, Radley left Shannon to start the house clearing and drove to the hospital. His appointment was filled with jargon and bad news hidden behind hopeful smiles. Medication was prescribed on a little yellow sheet signed in messy writing. A wad of paper was given to him regarding possible treatments, side effects, and how things were likely to progress over the next few months to years. And eventually, after a mandatory half hour delay, a twenty minute wait to fill the prescription, and a lecture from the pharmacist that the instructions were not to be taken lightly and 'do not mix with alcohol' was not merely a suggestion, it was over.

Radley didn't head straight for Uncle George's house. For longer than he took notice of, he sat in the car, staring out at the summer's day. People milled around outside the hospital. Some were waiting for the bus home, probably after appointments like his or visits to relatives. Others were wheeled in by paramedics straight to A&E. And all the while, the sun shone down on them all, not caring what anyone below was going through.

To Radley, it seemed fitting that he be sat there, isolated in his car, with a life sentence hanging over his head, whilst the rest of the world continued on with their own problems.

He was supposed to be with Shannon today. The plan had been for the pair of them to get the news of all his tests together, to hear about what the rest of his life would be like whilst they had each other to rely on. But fate, destiny, or whatever other crap enjoyed playing with them, had decided otherwise.

Radley scrubbed his face with a hand and sighed. He fumbled the key into the ignition and pushed the day's news to the back of his mind. There would be time later to worry about a life of medication. For today, he had to go support his wife as she cleared out the house of her last family member. If anything could distract him from the day, then clearing a house would be it.

The short drive there gave Radley enough time to smooth out the worry lines that decorated his face. A quick check in the rear view mirror told him he looked passable for a human being, even if there was a hint of wrinkling around his eyes.

As it turned out, it wouldn't have mattered if he'd walked in with tears still streaking down his face. Stacked in the hallway was enough stuff that he couldn't have seen his wife if he was seven feet tall and wearing heels.

"Shannon?" he called out. "Did you get buried in there?"

A voice sounded from the top of the stairs. "No, I'm still up here!"

He took two steps back so he was flat against the door, and could just see his wife's head sticking out around the banister. The sight eased away the rest of his worries with a laugh. Her hair was pulled back in a pony tail that had sent out tendrils to explore her face. And apparently in doing so had managed to cover her in dirt and dust.

"What do you want me to do?" he asked with a smile.

"Can you start in the living room? I'm almost done up here. That's the pile for the charity shop. There's a van coming in," she disappeared for a moment, "an hour, to take this lot away. Anything I'm keeping is still up here, but I can't get down there. So when they come, can you help take everything out to the van?"

Radley nodded, smiled, and said, "Sure. I'll start on the living room. You got your eye on anything in particular?"

A wide grin lit up Shannon's face. "There's a huge TV in there. It's unplugged, so check if it's working. If it is, we don't have to shop for one anymore."

"Will do. Anything else?"

"Whatever you think we need. If it's broken, there's a pile outside the back door to take to the dump. If we don't want it, it can go in the charity pile."

Radley nodded and headed into the living room. Sure enough, there was a flat screen the size he had dreamed about sitting in the middle of the room. Right in front of the chair Uncle George had always sat in.

First things first, Radley thought.

He found the plug for the TV easily enough, jammed it into the wall, and went in search of the remote. Two seconds later, he found it down the side of the chair. Instead of sitting in the chair that he had already decided needed to go on the dump pile if only for its hideous upholstery, Radley plonked down on the floor and set to checking the TV.

A bang from upstairs drew his attention for a second. Shannon's voice sounded, "I'm ok!" followed by a muttered explanation about dropping something.

Radley turned back to the television just in time to the last second of bright red eyes boring into him from the screen. No sooner had he leapt back away from the image, losing the remote in the process, than it disappeared, replaced by some holiday advert.

With his heart racing he took a moment to wonder what the hell sort of advert needed demonic eyes glaring at people. Probably some energy drink, he decided. Or one of those debt adverts.

The debtors are coming! he thought with a chuckle.

Retrieving the remote from where he dropped it, he flicked through a few of the channels. Everything seemed to be working. And as he was channel hopping, he could have sworn he saw the back end of the same advert again.

If it was a money problems advert, he thought, people would have a heart attack before the debtors got to them, seeing that.

He glanced behind him at the chair where Uncle George had died. Maybe that's what got him, too. But as soon as the thought crossed his mind, it was dismissed again at the thought of getting the ugly ass chair into the garden.

By the end of the day, Shannon had decided that house clearing was a lot more fun than moving house. After the first charity van had picked up half the house, she got real enthusiastic about throwing things out for the dump. All the sheets, bedding, the mattress, and every piece of outdated medicine in the bathroom got thrown into bin bags and dumped out the window onto the growing pile of things for the rubbish dump. All the furniture upstairs had been shipped off to charity to be cleaned up and resold to someone who needed it more than she did, and between Shannon and Radley, they'd gotten Uncle George's chair onto the grass out back.

In the car on the way back on the house, Shannon said, "We should have burned the thing."

"Yeah," Radley agreed, driving as slow as he could with a car full of stuff, "but that thing would have poisoned the whole street, for sure."

"It wasn't that bad."

He glanced over at her for a second. "Really? Did you ever see George *not* in that chair? He practically lived in it."

"Yeah, and I don't want to know how much he spilled on the thing."

"Exactly! We put a match to it, and it would take our heads off before we knew what was happening."

The pair laughed, but the moment was tinged with sadness.

As the laughter died, Shannon realised that she hadn't asked Radley how his hospital appointment had gone. Between hauling chairs and filling vans, she'd figured he would say something if it had been bad news. But hearing the edge to his laugh made her realise that even if he had received bad news, he likely would have kept it to himself until a better time.

But like the call about Uncle George's death, there was no good time to discuss negative test results, only varying degrees of bad.

Taking a deep breath, she said, "So you never told me how it went at the hospital."

Radley glanced away from the road, "Talk about it when we get home?"

Shannon nodded. They were only three streets away now.

But those streets seemed to stretch on forever. Every traffic light turned to red as soon as they got there. Several cars wanted to turn off the road and blocked traffic because they couldn't. What should have been a five minute drive dragged on for at least twice that. For Shannon it felt like an eternity.

Please, she thought to whoever might be listening, *don't let me lose him, too.*

The hunger came on quickly, bringing life and need back to the darkness. Senses reached out through an invisible network, tasting their surroundings, getting a feel for the lives of those it touched. Death sprang up everywhere like mushrooms blossoming in a forest. Not a place the darkness touched was devoid of it. The whole world stank of death. But those deaths were far away, teetering on the edge of a horizon that wouldn't come closer.

Deep in the world, where the darkness had fed last, the stench of a life near its end sang out. It begged to be tasted, to be caressed, and to be drained. The sickness called out to the darkness with such force, the rest of the world faded away to nothing.

In the dark the demon waited. Hunger tore a roar from its throat. Imminent death drew its lips into a sadistic grin that promised not only death but pain and torment.

***

"So it's not as bad as it could have been?" Shannon asked.

"Depends on what you mean. I'm still going to be taking this lot—" he held up the medication and gave it a rattle "—for the rest of my life. And the chances of us ever having our own kids…"

Shannon put a hand up to stop Radley talking. "You're not dying," she said. "That's the important thing. Kids and all that stuff, it doesn't matter. There are options."

"Yeah, but you always wanted your own."

"And?"

Radley tilted his head to the side and just looked at her. The intensity of his look clued Shannon in on why he was pushing this point so hard. "You expected me to leave you, didn't you?"

Radley blinked. "I… I've thought a lot about what this diagnosis would mean. And ever since we got married, you've wanted kids. For as long as I've know you, you've wanted kids. So, yeah, it crossed my mind that you might, you know, not want to stick around if I couldn't give you that." He looked down then, staring at his hands clasped in his lap.

Shannon couldn't help it. A great laugh erupted from her, startling Radley and making him look up. When she stopped laughing, Shannon thumped him on the shoulder.

"You, Rad, are an absolute moron."

Cue the blank stares all around.

"Oh, shut your moth!" Shannon said, a hint of a laugh still making her tone playful. "I've known you for how long? Six years, seven? And I've been in love with you for how long? Since about a half hour after we met? Do you really think I would even entertain the idea of leaving you?"

"I suppose not," he answered slowly. "But—"

"No buts. The only 'but' I want to see if yours crawling into the back of the car and dragging out all that stuff we brought home."

She stood up, and Radley came with her, wrapping his arms around her waist. "You're right," he whispered. "I am a moron. But you, you're an angel, if ever there was one. It's not going to be easy with the tablets and the side effects and the doctor's appointments. You know that, right?"

With a shake of her head, Shannon said, "Yes, I do know that. Now quit stalling and get your ass out to the car."

It wasn't until two weeks later that Radley spotted the back end of the advert and remembered about it. He was coming in from the kitchen with a plate of snacks when he caught a glimpse of two bright red eyes staring at him from the TV.

"Hey, can you rewind that?" he asked Shannon.

Since getting the almost-new telly set up in the living room, the pair had made it a point to watch a movie together once a week, this night being their third.

Shannon hit the rewind button. "What you looking for?"

"I'm wondering what advert those eyes belong to."

"What eyes?"

"The ones on that advert I just missed."

She hit the play button, and Radley sat down and placed the snacks on the table. Together they watched all the adverts before the movie, and not once did the eyes Radley had seen come up again.

"I must have imagined it," he said as the opening credits played across the screen.

"Isn't seeing things one of the side effects the doctor warned about?"

Radley settled in next to Shannon and answered, "Yeah, it is.

Must just be me, then."

Which was all well and good when said out loud, but the first time he had seen the eyes had been the day he picked up the TV from Uncle George's house. The very same day the doctor had prescribed the bevy of medication he was to take. So it must just be a side effect of the tablets. Except that he hadn't started taking them until the morning after clearing the house.

As the movie started to play, Radley's mind wandered to eyes as red as blood, and an uneasy feeling settled in his stomach. If the eyes weren't a side effect of the medication, it might be a new symptom from being ill.

With a deep breath and a steel willed determination, Radley pushed all thoughts of eyes and side effects out of his mind. In three days he and Shannon were off on a weekend break. It had been planned since before George's funeral, and two weeks on, they both needed it more than ever. A long weekend away together with no thoughts of eyes, death, or illness.

Perfect.

Tess loved nothing better than getting out of her parents' house for a weekend. Or two. Hell, she would give just about anything for her own place, but her job and income being what it was, the only places she could afford were bedsits that counted more in the kennel category than actual human housing. At almost thirty, she had managed all of six months living away from home. That had been thanks to her boyfriend at the time. They had been good together, great even, but it hadn't lasted. Six months, one week, and four days after moving out of her parents' house, Tess had been back on their doorstep in the rain asking if she could move back in.

Three years later, and it looked like she would die in her parents' house.

So when her friends called and asked if she wanted to house sit for them on their weekend away, Tess jumped at the chance. She had known both Radley and Shannon for years, having met them both about when they started going out. A couple of times the pair had offered their spare room to Tess as a way to get her out on her own. But for her it felt like going from one set of parents to another. Sure, there would be wild nights where the three of them drank whatever was in the house and passed out sometime around dawn. And there would no doubt be evenings of pizza and movies and more gossip that any one person could handle. But Shannon and Radley were a couple in love, and not only would that remind Tess of what she no longer had, but the pair would undoubtedly want to have private time away from prying ears.

House sitting, on the other hand, afforded Tess the luxury of her own place without the hassle of bills, food shopping, and insurance renewals.

"Go!" she told Shannon for the hundredth time. "I know where everything is. I know when you're back. I've got your number in case of emergencies. Go!"

"You sure…"

She didn't get to finish the sentence. With all the intention of a best friend, Tess shut the door on Shannon, all but forcing her out of the house. She waved at her friend through the half pane of glass and offered her a warm smile.

"Go!" she said again.

This time, Shannon turned away with a smile on her face and went for the car where Radley was waiting. Gingerly, Tess inched open the door, just in case Shannon came back to add something else to the list of 'if you need me.' She stood at the door, waving, until the car disappeared around the corner and her friends were gone.

Tess's first plan was a simple one: bake the pizza, crack open a bottle of wine, and settle in with the movie she had wanted to watch for weeks. The pizza was a simple throw in the oven and wait job. Whilst it bubbled away, Tess grabbed her glass of red and went exploring the house, carrying the kitchen timer with her.

Though she knew the house almost as well as her own, it was always new and exciting to see what had changed, and to confirm that she really was all alone. Not that Tess was a horror movie fan, but from the few she had seen, she knew that when house sitting, check the whole house. Wardrobes, cupboards, and even under the stairs, just in case. She also had a nosy streak in her a mile wide, and couldn't resist the lure of seeing what was hidden behind closed doors.

Some had called her rude for her snooping, and to an extent they were right. Had her intentions purely been those she told people when they found out, it wouldn't have been a problem. People generally, however, never believed the old argument of 'but if there's a break in while they're away, I need to be able to see what's missing.'

The timer dinged before Tess was done. Burnt pizza had never appealed to her, so she abandoned her search in favour of fresh pizza and a second glass of wine. She was here for the weekend, which left plenty of time for snooping.

One pizza and a glass of wine later, with the rest of the bottle sitting on the coffee table, Tess pressed play on the movie and settled in for the night.

***

In the darkness, hunger waited, growing more impatient by the day. Death was at its finger tips, and yet as the days passed, it slipped further away. Hunger made it impatience, eager to reach out and take whatever life happened to be near. The already dying were easiest, with their lives hanging in the balance between one moment and the next. The fear that was already imbued within them at their impending mortality made the death taste so much sweeter.

The darkness peered out from is hiding place to see what it could eat.

Fear made the flesh sweeter, but fear came in many forms, and tonight a feast was needed.

The movie had Tess confused. She thought she knew what it was about; a standard action movie with explosions, hot men, and guns. But every so often, a pair of red eyes flashed on the screen for a moment. At first she thought she had imagined it. Half a bottle of wine made the eyes go funny if all you've eaten is half a pizza. So Tess ignored it, concentrated on the movie, and poured another glass.

If she was already at the stage of seeing things, then what harm could the rest of the bottle do? she thought.

When they appeared again, Tess leapt out of her skin and spilled her wine down her front.

"Bloody hell!" she said.

Quick check of the sofa showed that the wine had only landed on her top. She put the glass on the table, and grabbed the remote so she could pause the movie and clean up. The second her fingers curled around the control, the eyes reappeared. This time it wasn't a glimpse and then gone in a second. It wasn't a brief flash of confusion that disappeared in an instant.

The eyes appeared, and this time, they remained.

The details didn't register at first. Tess just gripped the remote and stared into the eyes. Whatever action scene was playing out in the background faded away until all she could see was red eyes. Whilst her mind still functioned, she grabbed for her phone from the table and fumbled for the last number called.

Before she could get through, everything around her faded to black and filled with fire. The room around Tess ceased to exist. Darkness swallowed her whole and drilled its tendrils into every part of her. The only light she could see was the glowing red eyes filled with fire.

With nothing else to focus on, every terrifying detail of the eyes bored into Tess.

Instead of a single pair of eyes staring back, she now saw that each was made up of hundreds. Each tiny eye moved on its own, almost taking it in turns to stare deep into Tess. If she could have formed a thought it would have been that this pair of eyes was not just one thing living in the TV screen, but hundreds of the same things living in screens all over.

Her thoughts, however, didn't get past the primitive screams for help. Shouts for her limbs to move, to run, to scream for help, to do anything to get away from the darkness clawing at her skin.

But though her hands shook, they refused to move. Though her eyes streamed with tears, they refused to blink. Though her legs twitched, they refused to get up and run.

And then the pain began.

It spread through her like an unstoppable wave. Every inch of Tess burned with an agony that only grew, never faded. Her body twitched on the sofa, though she sat rigid backed and staring straight ahead. To anyone looking on, she was just sat watching the TV. Little about her outward appearance hinted at the fire that burned through her. And no one else would be able to see the eyes, even if they had been sat next to her.

No one could help her. Tess was as alone in death as she had been in the house not twenty minutes before.

And yet her mind was connected to every eye that stared back at her.

Her thoughts were reduced to that of a child hiding in the corner of a bed, huddled under the covers because something might be in the wardrobe.

Then, as suddenly as the pain had begun, it ripped away from her, leaving her body limp, her mind gone, and nothing but cold death in its place.

As weekends away went, Shannon couldn't have needed this one more. She abandoned her phone in the room the second she and Radley arrived, and didn't look at it again until they were on their way home.

"We should do that again," she said as she thumbed through her missed calls and messages.

Radley reached across the car and took her hand in his. "Yeah. We should. Next weekend?"

"I've got to work."

"Call in sick." He took his hand back to change gear and glanced over with a wink.

Shannon laughed, and for the first time in weeks it was a genuinely happy sound. "I've taken enough time off work lately. Hey, there's a message off Tess here."

She dialled her voicemail and started going through the options to listen to it.

"It can't have been important. I had my phone on me all weekend, and she never called it," Radley said.

Shannon went quiet in her seat. The voicemail started off silent, no greeting, and for a second she thought it might have been a hang up. Then the whimpering began. It was quiet at first, so quiet that Shannon thought she might be imagining it. As the message progressed, it grew louder, and eventually, Shannon could make out some words.

"The eyes," Tess whispered. "So many eyes."

Shannon frowned. "Either we're getting pranked," she said as the message continued in her ear, "or something's wrong."

"Let me listen?"

Shannon extended the phone so Radley could listen whilst he drove.

After a moment of listening, he said, "Eyes?"

Radley shook his head and went back to concentrating on the road. But Shannon had seen that look on his face before. It was the look he wore when he was thinking too hard, the same one he wore when he was trying to keep a secret.

"What is it?" she asked as gently as she could. She knew all too well that if she pushed him too hard when he had that face on she would get nothing from him.

"It's nothing."

"It doesn't look like nothing. You're gripping the wheel like we're about to crash."

He released his grip on the wheel, and glanced at Shannon with a smile. "Ok, so it's not nothing, but I don't think it's really anything."

"Which is your way of saying it is something but you don't want to tell me."

"Red eyes," was all he said.

Shannon stared at her phone and then back at her husband. "And?"

"I saw red eyes in the TV, remember?"

Shannon shook her head, a vague memory surfacing. "We don't know that Tess was in front of the TV when she called. She could have been anywhere." And even though she knew that was true, Shannon had the feeling that Radley knew what he was on about.

"Exactly why it could be nothing. Besides, she was probably just drunk and mumbling about some horror show she watched."

"Yeah, probably."

As much as Shannon wanted to believe that their friend had drunk one too many glasses of wine and dialled Shannon's phone by accident, something about the whole message seemed off. She looked down at her phone to see that she was still dialled in to her messages. Bringing the phone to her ear, she heard Tess's mumbling continuing until the message cut off.

Yeah, Shannon thought, *she must have called by mistake.*

Radley didn't know what to expect when he pulled up outside the house, but one thing was for certain, he couldn't get the image of those eyes out of his head. The first time he saw them he had dismissed them as an advert. The second time he thought he had been seeing things. But the voicemail from Tess had him on edge.

She drunk dialled Shannon, he thought over and over again.

Maybe if he could convince himself that what he saw was caused by stress or his imagination the sick feeling in his stomach would go away. The more he thought about it, however, the more nauseous he was about heading home. Until he was sure he would throw up the second he opened the door.

He didn't, and for that he was thankful. Shannon had been through so much in the last few weeks, that the last thing she needed was him parting with his lunch all over the drive.

The second Shannon opened the door, however, he wished he hadn't eaten at all.

Slumped over the end of the sofa was Tess. Her hair obscured her face, but it was obvious from the smell and the way she was so still that she was dead.

Shannon lurched out the door and threw up. Radley held still, forcing the bile back down through strength of will. The sound of Shannon retching made it all the harder. He turned away from the smell, closed the door, and put a hand on his wife's back.

He said nothing of the eyes that he saw staring out of the switched off TV.

Between police, paramedics, and a cleaning crew that did wonders on the living room, there had been more people in Shannon's house than the day they had the funeral for her Uncle George and held the wake there.

A heart attack is what Tess's death had been ruled as. She was younger than Shannon by almost three years. How could she have had a heart attack so young? It wasn't like she was ill or overweight. Tess had been friends with Shannon for years, and not once had she mentioned having any problems. Her parents were left shocked and devastated.

Shannon equally so.

The first thing she had done when the endless parade of flashing lights and officials was over was drag the sofa out of the house and order a new one. People had assured her that there wouldn't be any marks or smells on it once it had been cleaned, but all Shannon could see every time she saw it was her friend slumped over the arm, dead.

Images like that were what had Shannon waking in the night every night after coming home from her weekend away.

And it wasn't like that was the end of the things that could go wrong, either.

No sooner had Shannon and Radley been able to get back in the house, than he told her about the eyes he had seen staring at him out of the TV. Hungry eyes of red that no one else could see. It was then that the pair had decided against going to the police with the voicemail. After all, there was no proof that Tess hadn't drunk dialled them and then died afterwards.

Especially when no one but Radley could see the eyes.

He had even paused the television one time to ask if Shannon could see them.

She couldn't. But he could.

And now he saw them almost daily.

Shannon wasn't sure how much more she could take. First her mother a few years before. Then her last remaining family member. Now her friend. If death had any ideas on taking her husband, she was going to be ready, even if she had no idea what was happening.

In the darkness the demon slumbered. Death had filled its belly, but the creature was not satisfied. The fear running through the veins of its prey had been sweet enough, but the life had lacked the edge of sickness that gave the creature what it desired.

Sickness lingered close, however, and the demon stirred in the darkness. Hunger gnawed at its gut, twisting it into knots that begged to be loosened with the sweet taste of life being drained slowly, painfully. Great claws slashed at the dark with an eagerness that turned growls into laughing snarls. The more the demon fed, the more it wanted to feed, and now that it had tasted the flesh of the healthy, it wanted the sick more than ever.

Blood that rotted from within tasted so much sweeter than fresh youth. And now the demon knew its prey didn't have to be almost dead to be taken.

Try as he might, Radley hadn't been able to share his experience with the eyes with Shannon. Every time they popped up on the screen, he shouted, but she just couldn't see them. They had gotten far beyond thinking they were a part of his imagination. Not only because he had seen them before the meds started, but because the only place he saw them was in the TV. He might have been happy to believe his mind was playing tricks on him if the glowing red eyes had popped up in the bathroom mirror or the door of the microwave, or even the computer monitor, but there was nothing.

They weren't even haunting his sleep. Unlike Shannon, Radley's sleep was peaceful and undisturbed, just as his medication intended it to be.

And even though he saw the eyes daily, it didn't stop Radley from turning on the TV for their weekly movie night.

Just because I'm going crazy, he thought, *doesn't mean I should stop doing the things I like.*

"Honey, you coming to watch the movie?" he called. It was Shannon's turn to sort out the snacks.

She came through from the kitchen, and paused for a second before shaking her head and making her way to the new sofa.

Radley knew what she was seeing every time she came into the room; the same thing he did when he walked in. Their friend. They had talked briefly about moving, but neither of them wanted to go through that, not on top of everything else that had happened.

Snacks went on the table, and Shannon curled up at Radley's side. He hit the play button, and the movie started across the screen.

A second later, and the eyes were all Radley could see. Hundreds of them, thousands perhaps, all forced into the shape of a pair of eyes staring back at him. His breath quickened, hands clenching around the remote. His heart had never sounded so loud in his chest. So loud, in fact, that he swore he could hear the blood pulsing through him.

Somewhere in the back of his mind, Radley thought he should call out for Shannon. She was right next to him; couldn't she feel his heart flying free from his chest? Couldn't she hear his laboured breathing as he fought against the tide of agony that started in his head and inched towards his feet? Surely she could feel the heat that his body was throwing off in the wake of the fire?

But the longer the pain flowed, the quieter his thoughts on being saved became. No one could touch him in this moment. If his own wife couldn't see the eyes that were bleeding him dry, then how could she save him? How could anyone reach him and burrow deep enough into his mind to where the demon burned?

Was this how Tess felt? Radley thought. *Did she burn to death, too?*

It could have been hours or days since the eyes had appeared on the screen. Thousands of them all looking at him, all watching him, all determined to feast on his flesh and burn through his blood. A thousand eyes, a thousand deaths, a thousand wishes to be saved that would never be heard.

Except for one.

Somewhere, somehow, an angel must have been listening. That angel was Shannon.

Her face appeared as if from nowhere, between Radley and the TV screen.

"Radley!" she shouted. "Radley!"

He swallowed once, twice, and finally managed. "Yeah."

"We're getting rid of that damned TV."

Radley laughed. He couldn't help it. In the sudden absence of pain, he looked up at his wife, felt the sting of a slap he hadn't felt, and laughed.

"What the hell?" she snapped. "Why are you laughing?"

"I wanted a big screen TV."

It was the most absurd thing to say. He should have said thank you, I love you, you saved me, anything, but instead…

"I wanted a big screen TV. If I'd settled on the first one we looked at the first time we went shopping, we wouldn't have taken this one. We'd have sold it or given it to charity. None of this would have happened."

"What the hell even did happen?"

Wasn't that the question of the hour? Radley peered around his wife's shoulders at the TV. The eyes were gone, but he had a feeling it wouldn't last.

"I think our TV tried to kill me."

"The eyes," Shannon said with a huff. "How come you can see them and I can't?"

"I have no idea. And personally, I never want to find out. You're right, we're getting rid of this thing."

Shannon nodded, grabbed the remote that Radley was still gripping, and turned the thing off. She then got down on her knees and yanked out the plug.

"That's how we found it, isn't it?" Radley asked. "In Uncle George's house?"

"Yeah, it was." Shannon paused, plug in hand. "You don't think…"

Radley shook his head. "No. He was due a heart attack. Besides, we're not actually considering a killer TV are we?"

Shannon looked down at the plug in her hand, then back at her husband with a raised eyebrow.

Radley laughed again. "Yeah, I suppose we are. How about we skip the movie and go to bed?"

For the first time since the whole mess had started, Radley dreamed of a TV with glowing eyes, and somewhere in his dream he thought that whatever was in there was angry with him.

The next day he and Shannon drove out to the dump and left the TV there.

Disappointment was not something the demon was used to. When the darkness reached out for a meal, that meal was eaten. There were no interruptions or any other reason to stop feeding once the slaughter had begun. And yet in the darkness the demon prowled, unfed, hungry, and disappointed.

It was owed flesh, and one way or another it would feed.

Dinner came in the form of a man old for his age, with little sickness in him. There was no time to frighten him with images that would haunt his dreams and waking hours, there was only time to feed.

Fire poured through him, rooting him to the spot. No one came to rescue this man. He remained in the same spot as the demon fed, burning through him an inch of flesh at a time, drawing the process out. Every part of the demon spread the world over savoured this death, drinking down the blood and life offered to them.

In the end, with the man dead before it, the demon smiled. The darkness would forever remember the taste of the meal that got away, and with tendrils of its life planted the world over, one day it would find that meal, and when it did, death would not come quick.

The day after Shannon and Radley dropped their TV off at the dump they got a brand new, straight out of the box TV.

"Right," Shannon said, "Let's do this. But if you see eyes, we're taking it back and never getting another one."

"Deal."

On went the TV, and Radley sat down to stare at it.

There were no eyes that he could see, but he wasn't paying attention. The news was playing, and the top story was a worker who had been found dead of a heart attack in front of a stack of televisions in the dump. And sitting on top of the pile was their old one.

Other books by Michelle Birbeck

Novels

The Last Keeper (Book 1 in The Keepers' Chronicles)
Last Chance (Book 2 in The Keepers' Chronicles)
Exposure (Book 3 in The Keepers' Chronicles)
Revelations (Book 4 in The Keepers' Chronicles)

The Stars Are Falling

Short Horror Stories:

It Watches
Consequences
The Phantom Hour
Playthings
Zombie Lottery
A Glimpse Into Darkness (A Keepers' Chronicles Short Story)
Short Story Compilation:

- The Perfect Gift
- Isolation
- Never Go There
- Survival Instincts

About the author

Michelle has been reading and writing her whole life. Her earliest memory of books was when she was five and decided to try and teach her fish how to read, by putting her Beatrix Potter books *in* the fish tank with them. Since then her love of books has grown, and now she is writing her own and looking forward to seeing them on her shelves, though they won't be going anywhere near the fish tank.

You can find more information on twitter, facebook, and her website:

Facebook.com/MichelleBirbeck

Twitter: @michellebirbeck

www.michellebirbeck.co.uk

)